Classics (kind of)

William Shakespeare's
HAMLET

Adapted & Drawn
by Jason L. Witter

Classics (Kind of): William Shakespeare's Hamlet

ISBN-13: 978-1546455844
ISBN-10: 1546455841

First Edition: September 2017

witterworks1@gmail.com
www.facebook.com/witterworks
Instagram: @tiniest_vampire

This Ridiculous Book belongs to:

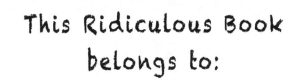

You are now
the proud owner of a
literary classic.
(kind of)

Dedicated to

Erin "Erni" Wolf

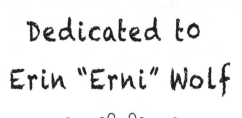

"If we are true
to ourselves,
we can not be false
to anyone."

- William Shakespeare, Hamlet

Special THANK YOU to the
Kickstarter Producers!

Christina Gonzalez
Daniel T. Cornish & Tiffani Cornish
Linus Loscher
Matthew & Charlotte Urbaniak
Nicholas Ganjei
Roger Smith

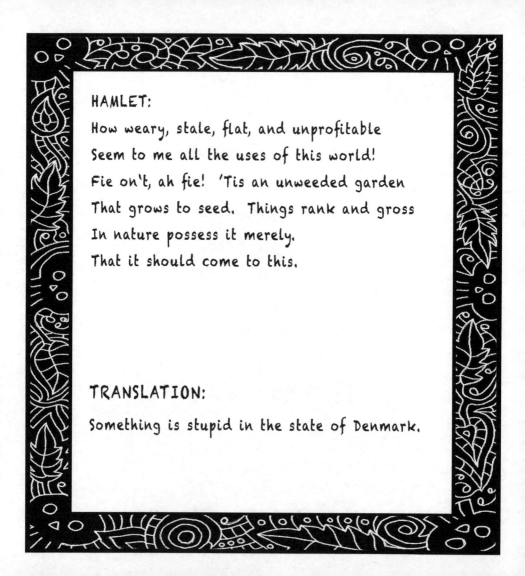

HAMLET:

How weary, stale, flat, and unprofitable
Seem to me all the uses of this world!
Fie on't, ah fie! 'Tis an unweeded garden
That grows to seed. Things rank and gross
In nature possess it merely.
That it should come to this.

TRANSLATION:

Something is stupid in the state of Denmark.

Hamlet is the grumpy prince of Denmark.

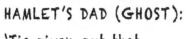

HAMLET'S DAD (GHOST):

'Tis given out that,

Sleeping in my orchard,

A serpent stung me.

So the whole ear of Denmark

Is by a forged process of my death

Rankly abused. But know,

Thou noble youth,

The serpent that did sting

Thy father's life

Now wears his crown.

TRANSLATION:

Your uncle killed me.

Hamlet's dad was napping in his garden, minding his own business, when stupid Uncle Claudius poisoned him to death.

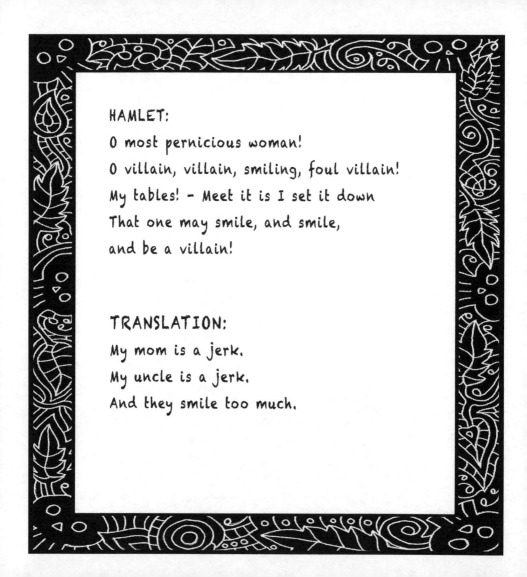

HAMLET:

O most pernicious woman!

O villain, villain, smiling, foul villain!

My tables! - Meet it is I set it down

That one may smile, and smile,

and be a villain!

TRANSLATION:

My mom is a jerk.

My uncle is a jerk.

And they smile too much.

GHOST DAD:
If thou didst ever thy dear father love -
Revenge his foul & most unnatural murder.

HAMLET:
The time is out of joint. O cursed spite,
that ever I was born to set it right.

TRANSLATION:

GHOST DAD:
Avenge me.

HAMLET:
Why me? This is lame.

HAMLET:

What a piece of work is a man!
How noble in reason, how infinite in
faculty! In form and moving how express
and admirable! In action how like an
angel, in apprehension how like a god!
The beauty of the world. The paragon of
animals. And yet, to me, what is this
quintessence of dust? Man delights not
me. No, nor woman neither...

TRANSLATION:

People are pretty cool. No, they're not.
I don't like people.

Hamlet doesn't know what to do, so he just wonders about things and acts like a weirdo.

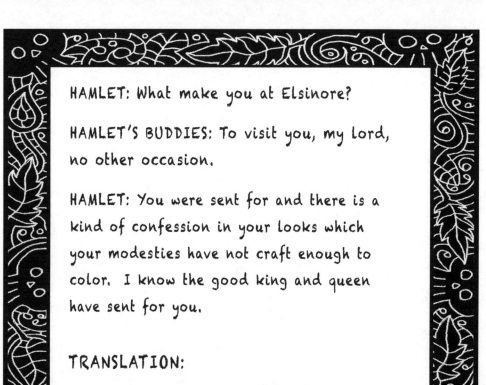

HAMLET: What make you at Elsinore?

HAMLET'S BUDDIES: To visit you, my lord, no other occasion.

HAMLET: You were sent for and there is a kind of confession in your looks which your modesties have not craft enough to color. I know the good king and queen have sent for you.

TRANSLATION:

HAMLET: Why are you guys here?

HAMLET'S BUDDIES: Just to hang out, bro.

HAMLET: You're fibbing. Stop fibbing.

Uncle Claudius doesn't trust Hamlet, so he brings in a couple of Hamlet's college buddies to spy on him, but Hamlet's too smart for that.

HAMLET:

To be, or not to be? That is the question -
Whether 'tis nobler in the mind to suffer
The slings & arrows of outrageous fortune
Or to take arms against a sea of troubles
And by opposing end them? To die, to sleep -
No more - and by a sleep to say we end
The heartache & the thousand natural shocks
That flesh is heir to - 'tis a consummation
Devoutly to be wished! To die, to sleep.
To sleep, perchance to dream, ay, there's the rub,
For in that sleep of death what dreams may come
When we have shuffled off this mortal coil,
Must give us pause.

TRANSLATION:

Is is better to be alive or dead? Uh... no idea.

HAMLET: I did love you once.

OPHELIA: Indeed, you made me believe so.

HAMLET: You should not have believed me, for virtue cannot so inoculate our old stock but we shall relish of it. I loved you not.

OPHELIA: I was the more deceived.

HAMLET: Get thee to a nunnery.

TRANSLATION:

HAMLET: Remember when I said I loved you? I was just kidding. Now go be a nun.

OPHELIA: You're a jerk.

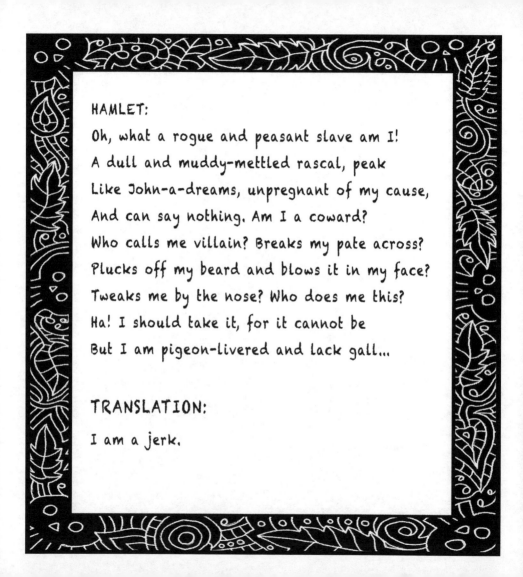

HAMLET:

Oh, what a rogue and peasant slave am I!
A dull and muddy-mettled rascal, peak
Like John-a-dreams, unpregnant of my cause,
And can say nothing. Am I a coward?
Who calls me villain? Breaks my pate across?
Plucks off my beard and blows it in my face?
Tweaks me by the nose? Who does me this?
Ha! I should take it, for it cannot be
But I am pigeon-livered and lack gall...

TRANSLATION:

I am a jerk.

HAMLET:

For murder, thought it have no tongue,
will speak with most miraculous organ.
I'll have these players play something
like the murder of my father
Before mine uncle. I'll observe his looks.
I'll tent him to the quick. If he do blench,
I know my course. The play's the thing
Wherein I'll catch the conscience
of the king.

TRANSLATION:

If Uncle Claudius doesn't like the play,
then I'll know he killed my dad.

OPHELIA: The king rises.

HAMLET: What, frighted with false fire?

HAMLET'S MOM: How fares my lord?

OPHELIA'S DAD: Give o'er the play.

UNCLE CLAUDIUS: Give me some light, away!

TRANSLATION:

OPHELIA: The king is standing up.

HAMLET: What's up with that?

HAMLET'S MOM: You okay there, guy?

OPHELIA'S DAD: Stop the play.

UNCLE CLAUDIUS: Get me outta here!

HAMLET:

Now might I do it pat.

Now he is a-praying.

And now I'll do 't.

And so he goes to heaven.

And so am I revenged.

That would be scanned.

No. Up, sword, and know thou

a more horrid hent.

TRANSLATION:

I could kill him now.

No, this isn't a good time.

Okay, I'll kill him later.

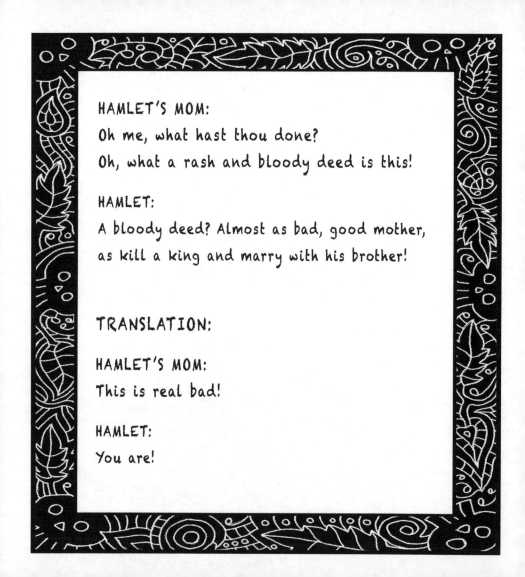

HAMLET'S MOM:
Oh me, what hast thou done?
Oh, what a rash and bloody deed is this!

HAMLET:
A bloody deed? Almost as bad, good mother,
as kill a king and marry with his brother!

TRANSLATION:

HAMLET'S MOM:
This is real bad!

HAMLET:
You are!

UNCLE CLAUDIUS:
When sorrows come, they come not single spies... but in battalions.

OPHELIA:
Hey non, nonny, nonny, hey, nonny...
You must sing A-down, a-down -
And you, Call him a-down-a - Oh!
How the wheel becomes it!

TRANSLATION:

UNCLE CLAUDIUS:
When it rains, it pours.

OPHELIA:
??????????

So, Ophelia goes crazy, sings some songs, gives everyone some flowers... and then she drowns.

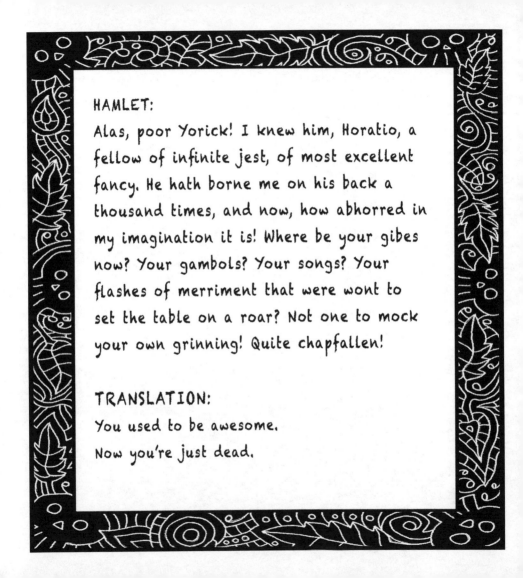

HAMLET:

Alas, poor Yorick! I knew him, Horatio, a fellow of infinite jest, of most excellent fancy. He hath borne me on his back a thousand times, and now, how abhorred in my imagination it is! Where be your gibes now? Your gambols? Your songs? Your flashes of merriment that were wont to set the table on a roar? Not one to mock your own grinning! Quite chapfallen!

TRANSLATION:

You used to be awesome.
Now you're just dead.

Ophelia's brother shows up, and he and Hamlet argue about who loved Ophelia more, and then Hamlet kills him in a sword fight involving a poisoned sword & poisoned wine... and it just gets totally nuts at this point.

Hamlet's mom dies.

Hamlet kills Uncle Claudius.

Hamlet wonders about a few more things.

Hamlet dies.

HORATIO:

Now cracks a noble heart.
– Good night, sweet prince,
And flights of angels
sing thee to thy rest! –
Why does the drum come hither?

TRANSLATION:

I'm sad. Later, dude.
Who's playing drums?

FORTINBRAS:
I have some rights of memory
in this kingdom,
Which now I claim my vantage
doth invite me.

TRANSLATION:
I guess I'm the king now.
How ya like them apples?

HAMLET:

The rest is silence.

TRANSLATION:

That's about the size of it.

Ham & Mac's Tiny Adventure

Hamlet & Macbeth

went to the Renaissance Fair.

When they arrived,

everyone got the heck outta there!

But Hamlet & Macbeth

did not really care.

They bought some balloons,

each ate a fried pear,

then Hamlet & Macbeth

decided they'd go again next year,

and maybe try the Tilt-A-Whirl...

if they dare.

Can you find 11 characters from "Hamlet"?

R	O	S	E	N	C	R	A	N	T	Z	W
O	J	I	M	B	O	B	I	G	M	E	R
B	A	R	N	A	R	D	O	E	O	Y	E
L	O	U	A	N	N	E	O	R	N	O	Y
G	U	I	L	D	E	N	S	T	E	R	N
H	A	R	R	Y	L	A	R	R	Y	I	A
O	P	H	E	L	I	A	I	U	P	C	L
S	T	E	V	E	U	L	C	D	B	K	D
T	I	T	U	S	S	U	E	E	P	O	O
Q	G	R	A	V	E	D	I	G	G	E	R

Can you help Hamlet get out of his head?

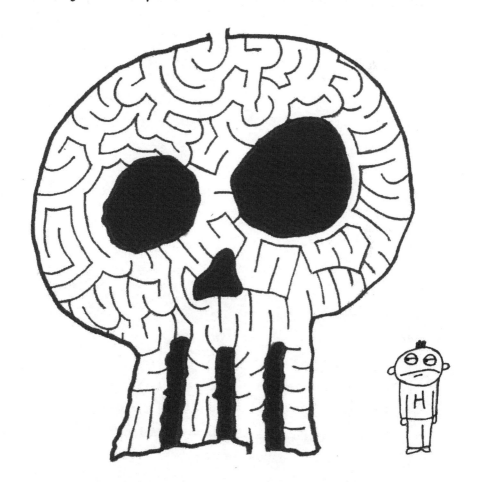

DOWN

1. Ophelia's brother (also the name of the father of Odysseus)
2. Richard _____, 1st guy to play Hamlet way back in the day.
4. Shakespeare was born in Stratford-upon- ____.
6. Ophelia's dad (was once played by Bill Murray).
7. Rosencrantz & Guildenstern are ____ (a play by Tom Stoppard).
12. "Dead Poets Society" star who played Hamlet - Ethan _____.
13. Hamlet tells Ophelia "Get thee to a _____."
14. "To be or not to be, that is the _____."

ACROSS

3. The _____ (Shakespeare's theatre)
5. Hamlet calls death "the undiscovered _____."
7. Hamlet is the prince of _____.
8. The Hamlet family castle.
9. Hamlet's dad died from poison in the ___.
10. Hamlet's good pal who, surprisingly, doesn't die in the play.
11. Occupation which Hamlet assigns to Ophelia's dad.
15. Hamlet's stupid uncle who causes all the problems.
16. Hamlet's mom who marries his stupid uncle.
17. "Alas, poor _____" - Hamlet says this to a skull.

Crosswords, words, words!!!

R	O	S	E	N	C	R	A	N	T	Z	W
O	J	I	M	B	O	B	I	G	M	E	R
B	A	R	N	A	R	D	O	E	O	Y	E
L	O	U	A	N	N	E	O	R	N	O	Y
G	U	I	L	D	E	N	S	T	E	R	N
H	A	R	R	Y	L	A	R	R	Y	I	A
O	P	H	E	L	I	A	I	U	P	C	L
S	T	E	V	E	U	L	C	D	B	K	D
T	I	T	U	S	S	U	E	E	P	O	O
Q	G	R	A	V	E	D	I	G	G	E	R

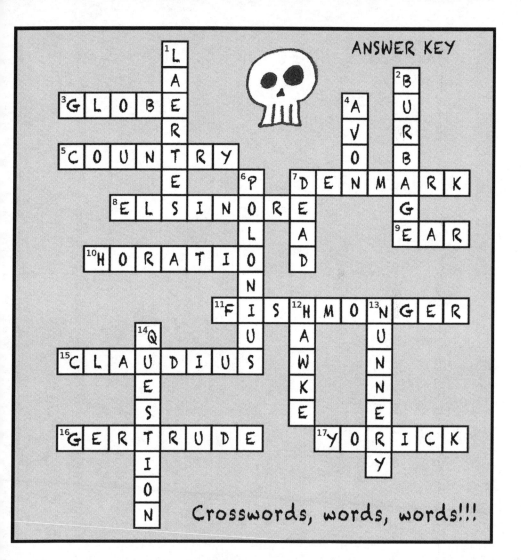

And now a HUGE THANK YOU to the "CLASSICS (kind of)" Kickstarter supporters!!!

Aaron S. Johnson, Abe Achkinazi, Alice, Alison Jackson,
Alyssa Peterson, Amanda Van Voorhis, Anastasia Thompson,
Andres Rodriguez, Andrew Jin Kim, Andrew Kottke,
Angelica Bernstein, Ann Book, Ann Pennington, Anonymous,
Arvon Villanueva, Asa Crowe, Ashley Spraggs,
Audrey & Tim Kirk, Avery Sill, baby panda, Beth & Ray Welt,
Beth McCloy, Blue, Bobbie Kirby, Bones, Bonnie Smith,
Brandy Artz, Brian Bhandey, Bryan H. Quackenbush,
Cal Godot, Chelsea Saul, Chris & Erin Damm, Chris Davis,
Chris Garner, Christina Gonzalez,
Christopher & Sarah Suski, Claire Heman
Corvin, Psyllus & Liam, Craig A. Butler, D. Marie,
Dan Purgert, Daniel T. Cornish & Tiffani Cornish,
Darcy Family, David C. Valdez, David Cherry
David Heitstuman, David W Hill, Deborah L Jarvis,
Delia Dubois CPA, Doskoi Panda, Duncan Laurence Bernard,
Elizabeth Hereford, Ella, Emery & Nicholas Faymoville,

Emily Lipkin, Erin & Ben Wolf, Ethan Kirkendall, FoolSinc,
George Simon aka "UG", Gracelynn, Hance Family,
Hans Fex, Hartbarger Family, Hongwoo Lee, Ian Aria,
J. Izzy Ladinsky, J.J., Jacob Jardel,
James & Tammie Classen, James Poulette, Jami Ann Kravec,
Jamie Vigliotti, JayPear & SarePear, Jennifer Greer,
Jennifer Wilson, Jess Farnsworth, Joan & Andrew,
Joanna Furgal, Joseph Bond, Jp LaFond,
Justin & Kendra Hutchison, Karen Kelley, Kari Monster,
Kaytlin & Kalysta Tumlinson, Keebler Hammons, Kevin Ferrin
Kyra & Thomas Richter, Lance Lorenz, Laura Packer
Lee Francis IV, Lee Mann, Leonard & Jane Witter,
Linus Loscher, Lisa, Lisa Sustaita, Lon Cook,
Lori & Russell Stewart, Lucas Homlish, Lucy Loonan,
Mae Diseth, Maggie S, Maria Friesen, Marilyn Howard,
Mark J. Frederick, Mary Danish, Mary Hillhouse,
Matthew & Charlotte Urbaniak, Meredith, Mia,

Mike "Superman" Wilson, Molly A. King, MOOTS
Morgan, Tiffany, Shayla, Ian & Keira, Nadia Heller,
Nathan Erickson, Nic Sage, Nicholas Ganjei, Noor Iqbal,
Norwitz Family, Olivia DeLoach, Patrick Nix, Peter Howard,
Peter Mazar, Peter Parker, R P Steeves, Rafael Rossi,
Randy Ditton, Rob G Fowler, Roger Smith, Russell Family,
Ryan Denmark, Samantha Jo-Ann Shuma,
Sandra Karolus-Mikhael, Sarah Vetter, Scottie & Pepper,
Sevrina Flores, Shane, Miranda & Esme Magnusson,
Shannon Keller, Shannon Stanfield, Shawn Bean "M3ATSICLE"
Shehan Jayasekera, Stacy Cantwell, Steve "The Bard" Latour,
Sylvia Flores, Terri the Terrible, Tesche, The Donuts,
The Filipovichs, Tina Benjamin, Title Wave Books
Toby Selbee, Tom Backus, Tricia Sachs,
Vanessa, Lynn & Tony Akins, Winston Kou, Yang-Chieh Lee,
YettiChild, Yu, Yvette Alvarez, Zack Newman,
Zackary Collins

"All the world's a stage,
and all the men and women
merely players.
They have their exits
and their entrances,
and one man in his time
plays many parts..."

- William Shakespeare

TRANSLATION:
We're all actors! Yay!

William Shakespeare was born in 1564 in the small village of Stratford-upon-Avon in the United Kingdom. Having written such plays as Hamlet, Pericles, Timon of Athens, Henry VI Parts I to III, and King John, Shakespeare is generally considered to be the greatest playwright the English language has ever known. His plays have been translated into 75+ languages, and countries around the world perform his plays ever year, every month, every week, every day!

Jason L. Witter once played Messenger # 2 in a community theater production of "Antony & Cleopatra."

Made in the USA
Columbia, SC
02 December 2017